i

The Community Writers

Book cover photos was taken by Carol Wideman and Willie Wideman of the Dorchester, MA areas.

Copyright @2022 by Friends of the Uphams Corner Library, Inc. February 2022

ISBN:978-1-7332846-1-5

A Writer's View Anthology

Short Stories, Essays and Poems

The Community of Writers:

Dorchester Community Writers

And

B.Fit! Community Writers

ACKNOWLEDGEMENTS

This is the Friends of the Uphams Corner Library's second anthology. This book came out of our second workshop project, "How to Write a Short Story."

Thanks to Authors Without Borders.

Thanks to Colleen L. Roberts, Marva Martin and Michele Saunders for editing this book.

Special thanks to all our Contributors that took the time to share their journeys and poems.

CONTENTS

The Community Writers

The instructors of "How to Write a Short Story"

 Willie Wideman-Pleasants

 Vickie Wideman-Victor

 Colleen L. Roberts

The Community Writers

Photo by Vickie Wideman

Three dogs and Broken Bones

by

Smiler Q. Wooten Haynes

As a true Cancerian, I married the boy I met in high school and moved to Boston. We lived with relatives until we found a place of our own.

I loved being home for our children, Arnetha, Anjela, Randy Jr. and Kipling. I always served a tasty hot dinner when my husband, Randy Sr. came home from work. We all ate together.

You would think, having four children and a wonderful, hardworking meat cutter for a husband; two dogs (a Chihuahua, and a mutt); a rabbit and a parakeet was enough to keep me busy at home.
Not me!

I took on more work by designing and altering clothes for my customers in my sewing room. My cutting-edge styles were on Billboard, Ebony magazine, and New York World's Fair as well as many fashion presentations all over New England. I did this for fifteen years.

I chose this career path when I won a state-wide 4-H competition in the eighth grade in West Virginia. My winning garment was made out of a feed sack. Yes, feed sack.

For ten years I produced the very popular *Fun and Fashion Revues,* as well as donated my fashions to the community. The models were fabulous. Shelly Knox; Domingo Andrade; Yvonne Willis-Rose; Lionel Kelly; and many others as well as the Frank Hatchett Dancers from New York and Springfield, Massachusetts.

Well, in the summer of 1976, I was about to accomplish my lifelong dream of opening my own fashion design boutique in the Back Bay of Boston on Gainsborough Street, one block from the world-famous Symphony Hall.

A week before my boutique opening my daughter Anjie, who lived in Framingham, was going on vacation and needed a dog sitter. The dog was a beautiful large, red Springer Spaniel named Chipper. I took Chipper for a walk. Chipper was so happy to get out in the open, she took me for a run and dragged me to the curb on

Stanwood Street. Unfortunately, this event caused me to break my right hand.

My shop opened with the help of my sister, Dreama. (I couldn't have done it without her). With right hand in a cast, I sewed the clothing with my left hand. I hired skilled workers from Iran, Barbados, and the Virgin Islands to help me. I catered to such well-known people as Lotsa Poppa; Commodores; Tavares; and Trammps as well as fashioned wear for weddings and proms. I even had lunch with Sammy Davis Junior at the Freedom House.

Some years later, my granddaughter Vanessa and I were walking her dog Jake on Stanwood Street. A muscular black rottweiler suddenly attacked Jake after breaking out of his yard. I grabbed a nearby trash can and fought the dog off of us. As the rottweiler was restrained, I realized that in the process of saving Jake, I broke my right pinkie finger! I was eighty years old at that time. Two weeks later, with finger in a cast, Jake pulled me down a flight of stairs, into my yard while trying to chase a squirrel. I broke my left arm and broke my shoulder in

```
```

three places. I was hospitalized and operated on and put in a big cast. I was unable to live independently. My daughter, Arnetha and her significant other, Michael, took good care of me in their home for six weeks.

I have osteoporosis and I have broken other bones. One time I was in a car accident on the corner of Brunswick Street and Blue Hill Avenue. My husband was driving and collided with another car and broke my collarbone. Another time I was on the beach in Panama when I slipped on the Astro Turf. What a trip!!!!

It is the year 2021 and all is well. I am 88 years old, working as a professional print model in catalogs, advertisements, brochures, etc. I act as an extra in movies with such stars as Denzel Washington, Jada Pinkett Smith, and Jennifer Lawrence. I also volunteer as a reading coach at my church. *No dressmaking, no fashion shows, and no dogs.*

My granddaughter Vanessa met the love of her life and moved out of the state with Jake. They live happily with my three beautiful great-grandchildren.
No JAKE. DOG GONE!!!

A Friend Knows
by
Beulah Meyers

"Soon as Monday rolls around again I got to put all that partying to an end." Dena sings along to the lyrics of "Livin' for the Weekend," one of her favorite songs on the radio by The O'Jays, as she drives to work. Music always puts her in a good mood. She thinks to herself, "Bout time this funky mood I've been in all weekend finally swung right instead of left."

As Dena pulls into the parking lot, she glances at the clock on the dashboard of her car, "Damn, I got three minutes to spare, and a parking spot right up front. Good start for Monday morning."

Dena checks her make-up and hair in her visor mirror, "Too much gray showing. Time for a touch-up, but what the heck, still good enough for this place."

She grabs her tote bags, rambles through one of them and finds her ID. She exits the car and walks toward the entrance door. When Dena reaches the glass door, she pauses for a second and checks out her reflection in its glass.

As Dena enters the building her mood automatically swung from right to left. To Dena, the entire workspace feels like an after-thought. Her desk is too low to properly accommodate the computers and monitors. The temperature inside the building is always unstable, being either too hot or too cold. Her work group cubical walls are waist high compared to all the others in the entire building. No privacy, you can't even scratch without someone seeing it. Dena often would say to her friend and co-worker Shanna, "It feels like a fishbowl in here and most of these folks act like strange fish. They feed on other people's weaknesses with verbal intimidation and they revel in the misfortune of others." Especially Dena's supervisor, Jane.

Dena heads straight to her desk positioned directly across from her friend Shanna. She puts her bags down and sits at her desk.

"Morning Shanna, how are you doing today?"

"Hey girl, it's about time you dragged in here."

"How are you doing?"

"Much better before I came through that door," Dena retorted.

Shanna is attractive and always neat in her appearance. She and Dena get along well, and occasionally get together during off hours. They are often seen at work whispering, laughing and sharing gossip.

"Shanna, what did you do this weekend?

"I went to the theater and I caught this really good movie." Shanna said with smile.

"What was it about?" Dena queries as she wheels herself over to Shanna's desk to hear all the details. They both begins to laugh and chat about the details of the movie, when Shanna taps Dena's arm and whispers to her, "Dena, look up." Dena lifted her head and sees a large figure of a women moving in their direction. Her tight-fitting slacks sits about three inches above her flat, brown shoes that revealed her white socks. The woman's brown, lifeless hair could have used a good stylist or at least a good washing.

Jane, Dena's supervisor, is now standing in front of Dena. Dena thinks to herself, "What does this bitch want?"

"Dena, is your work finished?" Jane asked sheepishly.

Dena looks up at Jane with a huge frown on her face. Her body tenses up, with her brain now in a battle with itself trying hard not to say out loud what she really thinks.

"Jane, when is the work ever finished?" Dena responded. She rudely continued, "Why are you asking anyway? Is it because you see me talking to Shanna?"

Dena's voice gradually got louder, directing her one-way rant squarely at Jane. Dena lobbed another criticism at Jane, "Why are you here Jane? This is not kindergarten, nor grade school. You don't get to tell me when or where I can speak!"

As Jane quietly begins to walk away, Dena stands and begins to walk behind Jane, and continues her rant. "I don't know why you came over here, I think you need to find your way back to your desk!"

When Dena stood up and started to move in Jane's direction, Shanna reached and grabbed Dena's arm. Dena stopped moving, and stopped ranting. She turns back, smiles at Shanna, sits down in her chair and wheels back to her desk mumbling to herself, "Mood swing, you went left, but if you don't swing to the right again, it's going to be a long day.

Dena was thankful to have a friend who could recognize when she was about to make a big mistake.

MY LIFE

by

Bernice Wideman

The school was Kinterbish High and the year was 1955. During those times, segregated schools were the norm. Bernice was in the 11th grade and on the girls' basketball varsity team. At first, her father did not want her to play. Mr. Treadgill, the coach promised her father that he would make sure no harm would come to her especially when they had night games. He convinced Bernice's father to allow her to play. Bernice's mother had unquestionable belief in her talent which gave the green light for Bernice to pursue the sport. Mr. Treadgill had his winning team.

Bernice loved basketball and spent her time practicing and being the best possible player. The game of basketball was her enjoyment.

Bernice was one of the major players on the basketball team. She never thought of herself as a star, but as a good basketball player who loved the game.

Secretly, she wished that she could somehow compete professionally as a female player. For Bernice it was an unrealized dream.

Some of the players on her team were Olivia, Dora Mae, Corean, Lorean, and others. "We were the point guards." Bernice proudly said.

Bernice was the shortest. She played as if she was six feet tall. The team members all complemented each other as they controlled the court. They beat teams like York West End and the high school in Meridian, Mississippi. The school team even advanced to a few championships.

Bernice remembered a particular incident that happened one night that could have threatened her ability to play.

"It happened on our way home from one of our night games in Meridian, Mississippi. Our driver T.L., a senior, who drove our team bus, The Blue Goose, decided to take a detour right up to the State Line, a night club that sat on the border between Alabama and

Mississippi. It was about 10 PM and we had no idea why T.L. had stopped. He jumped off the bus and said nothing. All I could think about was that, if my father found out, I would not be allowed to play anymore."

Luckily, for everyone involved, the coach was driving shortly behind the bus in his car. Bernice remembered that Mr. Treadgill boarded the bus left his car overnight and drove the bus to drop them off.

Bernice graduated 1957. It was hard leaving the best two years of high school to venture into a labor force that did not advance nor acknowledge Black talents.

Bernice had heard stories about the Blacks that had been persuaded by the Great Migration movement (between 1917 to 1940 Blacks left the South in droves to such Northern states as Illinois, Michigan and Massachusetts.) for safer lives and better jobs.

When Bernice graduated high school, domestic work, working in the mills and fields were the majority of jobs available to Blacks in the south, except for a few Blacks that could afford college.

A Writer's View

There were multiple unjust systems created to keep Blacks enslaved to manipulation and in debt including Jim Crow laws. White land owners cheated the Black farmers, underpaid the cotton pickers ($0.01- 0.02 per pound) which kept Blacks in debt. Some Blacks could barely read or write which left them vulnerable to the Jim Crow Laws.

The horror of Blacks being forbidden to seek better wages were real. Blacks were charged with vagrancy and jailed for free labor by a correctional system. They were beaten, raped, hung, and sometime burned beyond recognition. Jim Crow laws were the manifestation of angry white southerners who wanted to maintain their labor force by fear.

It was no wonder Bernice thought of leaving when she finished high school.

Bernice worked for a short time as a domestic worker in Mississippi. But there came a time when she was approached by a recruiter to be a live-in maid in the North which gave her an opportunity to leave home.

Bernice was given traveling money and a bus ticket to Great Barrington, Massachusetts. The recruiter gave her a place to stay until she was assigned to a family.

Bernice stated, "The first family lived on Mohegan Drive in Connecticut. I was there living with a white family who had two children, in a neighborhood of white doctors and lawyers. I was given my own bedroom with a small TV, a rocking chair which I enjoyed while watching, 'All My Children,' my favorite soap opera."

Bernice felt a little uncomfortable because of the husband's inappropriate flirtations, but she refused to let it bother her because he had not touched her.

Months later, one evening, the unspeakable thing happened. Bernice said, "I came down stairs after finishing my upstairs cleaning. I had planned to go to my bedroom, sit in my rocking chair and enjoy my TV dinner. With food in hand, I went to my bedroom, turned the light on and there was the husband lying in my bed with all of his clothes off."

Bernice dropped her plate turned and ran out of the house screaming. She ran to the house next-door where another maid, her friend Martha lived and worked. The neighbor allowed her to use her phone to call the recruiter. Martha went back over to the house with Bernice. Bernice packed her clothes in the new trunk she had just purchased. The recruiter told her to get a room at the YWCA until they could find another family for her.

After a few days Bernice was placed in another home in Hartford, Connecticut. The lady of the house was a lawyer. Bernice explained to her why she had left the other residence.

The lawyer explained, "I would love to take your case but we will not win, because you are Black, no one would take your word against a white man. They would think you were after his money. But what I will do is make sure no live-in maid works for that family."

Bernice and Martha found an apartment that they shared until Martha decided to go back to the South to get married.

In 1965, Bernice moved to Boston where her brother, Peter, and sister, Idella lived. She went back to school, earned her Licensed Practical Nurse's license and worked for Children's Hospital for over forty years, during that time she raised three sons.

Years later Bernice went back to Great Barrington, Massachusetts to see how the area had changed.

She noticed that it was the same small rural area with shops. She looked for the house where she first stayed when she arrived in Great Barrington, but could only remember that it sat on a hill. Bernice saw a house on the hill just outside of town, but was not sure if it was the same place.

Bernice, a Black woman from the South, had a religious drive to do good; a social drive to fit into society; a drive to better herself through education; and a nurturing drive to raise a family. She has travelled the world on cruise ships of every port and even the Hawaiian Islands. She organized trips, mostly in the

United States, Bernice did fundraisers for her Eastern Star family and helped to sponsor food drives for the homeless.

She experienced the sadness and goodness the world offered, and she also found time to help and inspire others.

Below are two of her basketball team members:

Corean Johnson-Williams (2022)

Olivia Wilson (2022)

Artist: Willie Wideman

Kia and Her Football

Kia and Her Football

by

Dorothy Wideman

Kia is a perky, happy ten-year-old girl, who wears a bang and two braids. She has been passionately rooting for her favorite football team, the New England Patriots!

Every year since she was eight years old, Kia looks forward to football season. Kia understands the words antagonist and protagonist. She sees school as the antagonist when it comes to reading, writing, and learning math. Football season is the protagonist because it gives her joy at school.

Kia's Sunday routine is wearing her favorite football team shirt and helmet. While watching her team play, she eats chips and dip, drinks soda and munches on a cheeseburger with ketchup, mustard and a sweet pickle on the side.

During each football game Kia would aggressively yell at the players on the TV screen. "That was a bad throw! You want me to suit up and throw the ball?" When her team would lose a game, Kia would say, "No problem. Get'em next time." But when they would win a game, she would say, "A little closer to the Superbowl!"

Kia's parents are invested in her life. Mom is a part-time teacher and a full-time mother. Dad is a full-time accountant and a full-time father. They live in a single-family Victorian house just outside of city limits.

Mom and Dad noticed Kia's mood had changed from not liking schoolwork to liking schoolwork during football season. They even received positive reports from her teachers:

Kia sits with her peers during lunch time and plays with her classmates during recess. She raises her hand in class and her homework is done on time.

Her parents wondered how they could help Kia keep that same energy and motivation about schoolwork after football season is over.

Before every Sunday game, Mom, Dad and Kia would prepare to enjoy the game. Dad would make cheeseburgers on grills outside in the cold weather. Mom would get the chips and dip on a tray and Kia got the sodas out of the refrigerator. Once the football game preparation was finished the family would wait in the living room for the game to start.

Kia's parents asked her why she seemed happier and more energetic during football season than during the other times of the year. Kia replied, "I get more attention and support from everyone during football season. The kids at school like how I give them information about how to play football and the different positions. I teach them how to keep score and how to update all the wins and losses data. The kids ask me personal question about football players, and I know the answers! The teaches were excited when I talk about football."

Kia paused for a few seconds then looked at her

parents and said, "You make sure I have my special things to eat during the football games. You say how nice I look in my shirt and helmet and how you like me during football season."

"Wow!" her parents said with a surprised look on their faces.

"Thank you for sharing your feelings," Mom said, "We love you all the time and all year round."

Dad replied, "Kia! After football season is over, I want you to pick something else you are passionate about and keep that same energy, excitement and enthusiasm."

"Kia, on your next project, pick a special meal and some favorite clothing to wear to help you enjoy" Mom said. All three looked at each other, smiled, hugged, sat down and watched the game.

Kia- '2021'

Survival
by
Alberta Sequeira

What actually is survival? It's defined by the dictionary as "to remain alive after the death of someone; the cessation of something; or the occurrence of some event; and our need to continue living. Survival depends a great deal on a person's ability to withstand stress in emergency situations. Your brain is without doubt your best survival tool. It your most valuable asset in survival. Mental skills are much more important than physical skills in survival situations.

I'm sure all of us have had to survive after some sort of tragedy in our lives. It can happen in our childhood, teenage years or adulthood. Those with weak mental strength to move on after a tragedy are lost in life.

I found out with the losses I had experienced with loved ones that with my faith and deep connection to God, I have survived; not happily, but with finding peace. My first heartbreak was the loss of my father, Brigadier General Albert L. Gramm, who had been one of the

Army's commanding officers during WWII fighting in the battles of Metz, Lorraine, and the famous Battle of the Bulge. He died of cancer at eighty years old.

I waited too long to take the time to know this wonderful man as a soldier. Questions were held back thinking there was time to ask. He had more to explore than I had realized.

Death of a parent is something we brace ourselves for but never want to face. My mother, Sophie Gramm, died at ninety-two, from a stroke. It's never easy once we lose both.

Another pain I survived was losing a mate. I lost my husband, Richard Lopes, when he was forty-five from cirrhosis of the liver at the Veteran's Administration Hospital in Providence, Rhode Island from his years of drinking beginning when he was a teenager. This young, gentle-man whom I had married turned into someone I didn't know. This alcoholic demon overtook him like it had done with past family members; from generations down to generations. I survived many beatings during his blackouts.

I became a great enabler for fourteen years. This was way too long dragging my two beautiful daughters through the stress and fears. I joined the statistics of divorced couples from alcohol abuse so I could survive after a breakdown pushing myself beyond what I could take mentally and physically trying to help him recover.

The worst agonizing pain of loss is with a child. No matter how young or old, their loss is one that is supposed to happen after their parents die and not before. There are no words to describe this survival.

I watched my daughter, Lori, who had been a happy, loving, funny girl who enjoyed life and her family, slowly turn into a lost soul who refused to hold onto professional help. The demon had a tight hold on her causing her to follow in the same footsteps as her father. I heard her take her first breath at birth, and her last when life-support had been taken off her. I never thought the tears would stop but I held tight to the love of God, knowing He was all Merciful and Loving.

Lori was buried with her dad at the St. Patrick Cemetery in Somerset, Massachusetts. They are facing a huge statue of the Blessed Mother with her arms out wide; the one that gave Lori peace knowing Our Lady was watching over her father.

What was I going to do with this pain? I reached out to other substance abusers at halfway homes, rehabilitation centers, court-ordered programs, jails, colleges, libraries, and any place that welcomed my talks. I needed to plant the seed of survival knowing God would do the rest.

For a woman with weak knees to speak in public, I continued to become a director, producer co-host to the NBTV-95 Cable TV show, a co-founder to Authors Without Borders, and a writer for the Cape Cod Today blog with informative articles on alcohol and drug addiction. I even started workshops for writers to tell their stories.

I became an author who wrote about Richard in *Someone Stop This Merry-Go-Round; An Alcoholic Family in Crisis* and the sequel with Lori in *Please, God, Not Two: This Killer Called Alcoholism*. I needed to know what else I could have done differently to help Richard and

Lori so I wrote *The Mindset of The Alcoholic and Drug Addict*. I had thirty-four alcoholic and drug users tell their stories on what does and doesn't work in substance and alcohol abuse recovery and what they need from their families. My survival is through the help of God to reach out to others going down a path of death with addiction.

How do we survive tragedies? We work through them. We can't bypass grief in life. Allow yourself to grieve. We have to go through the process to heal. Release your pain with tears, anger, guilt, depression, and finally come to accept what has happened and move on the best we can.

I found that helping others instead of concentrating on my loss, has helped me. No, we don't heal as people think if we write about the experience. We learn with God's help to move on with what He puts in front of us. As they say, "Put one foot in front of the other" or "One day at a time." (alberta.sequeira@gmail.com)

The Wedding Necklace

by

Colleen L. Roberts

Sheila Thompson smiled at her reflection, admiring the diamond encrusted heart of her new necklace as it lay upon her honey-brown skin. She had chosen it especially for today. Her best friend Grace was getting married and at their middle age that was something to celebrate.

"Mama," her college-age daughter Pam called.

"Are you awake? I made breakfast."

"Come in, baby," she said. She glanced at Pam's reflection in the mirror. "How do you like my new necklace? Is it snazzy enough for the Maid of Honor to wear?" she laughed.

"It's beautiful, Mama."

"You don't sound too impressed. What is the matter with you? Ever since you came in yesterday you've been moping around like you lost your best friend."

Pam spread her slim, ebony body across Sheila's bed. "I don't feel right about this wedding."

"Why not?"

"Auntie Grace shouldn't be marrying Lamont."

"What are you talking about? They love each other, which is all that matters."

"I know." Pam got up. "I'll be in the kitchen." Sheila shook her head and went back to the necklace, but Pam's words haunted her. Grace's man Lamont Grier had always been a fixture around her house, doing handy work and taking care of the lawn ever since Pam was small. He even babysat sometimes when she had to work long hours at the office. He was there when Pam graduated from kindergarten, sixth grade, eighth grade and finally high school. He cheered her on when she wanted to do boys football and even though she wasn't allowed to play, he kept her positive and said she might get the chance someday. He was the only decent Black man Pam had ever known.

"She ought to be happy for Lamont instead of saying things like that," she said to her reflection. "I am."

But even as the words slipped from her mouth, Sheila felt a strong check in her heart. A gray shroud rose up inside and made even the gold and diamond heart seem dull and lifeless. She knew the truth. She knew the moment he entered her heart and made himself at home, but she let him go. Other things had become more important. She touched the necklace.

"Mama, Auntie Grace and the limo are here," Pam called from the porch an hour later.

"I'm coming," Sheila shouted from behind her bedroom door. She zipped her lavender and gold bridesmaid dress in a suit bag and picked up the hat box. She looked in the door-length mirror. Her face was smooth, her lips full but not fat. Sheila turned a few times to catch a glimpse of her slender body.

"Well alright, you go girl," she said aloud and laughed.

"Mama, hurry up."

"I'm coming." She gave Pam a kiss as she flew by her. "I'll see you later, baby."

"Wait," Pam said.

Sheila turned at the door and looked into her daughter's serious face. "What is it, Pam? I have to go."

Pam's brows wrinkled. "He's marrying the wrong woman. You know it."

"Stop it, girl."

"Lamont loves you. And you know good and well you love him. How could you let this happen?"

Sheila turned away. She felt grayness close in around her spirit as she went to the car where Grace was smiling from ear-to-ear, her head filled with rollers.

Grace did a little screech as she hugged her. "It's finally happening, girl," she said. "I'm marrying the most wonderful man on Earth."

"Oh, really? What about Denzel?"

"He's a close second." She giggled.

She settled back into the deep cushioned seats as Grace talked on and on about the ceremony and celebration. She smiled and nodded, trying to feel the happiness she saw in Grace's face. But all she could feel was her daughter's words. She wished Pam was not so straight forward and that she'd learn to keep some things to herself. She gazed out the car window, watching her city fly by. They even passed the bank where she'd worked for ten years. Her blood, sweat and tears filled the place from the mailroom to the executive suites on the sixth floor. She could see the whole city from her office and often felt like she owned it. What a victory getting that office was. But there she'd begun to lose her life in steady drops. When she realized what had happened, it was too late.

"Sheila," Grace said.

Sheila jumped. "What?"

"We're here. Where have you been for the past ten minutes?"

She smiled and followed her friend into the church dressing rooms. She couldn't let Grace know how she was feeling. She had never seen her friend so happy.

The bridal party, Grace's mama and other assorted relatives were already there. Sheila gave a shout to the whole group at once.

Grace's mother, Georgia Tucker, came up to her. "How you feeling today, Sheila?" she asked. She put an arm around her shoulders.

"Fine," Sheila said and tried to move away but Georgia tightened her hold and carried her to a quiet corner of the dressing room. "I want today to be perfect for Grace. She's waited a long time for this and she's got a good man. Don't spoil it for her."

"Why would I? Grace is my best girl."

"I'm just saying. I know how close you've been to Lamont and I know how hard it must be to let him go. He belongs to Grace now so you just have to accept that. Don't cause any trouble, hear?"

"Yes, ma'am."

Georgia's wide, toothy smile and firm squeeze sent chills through her body. As she prepared her hair and put on her make-up, she felt the ominous warning under

Georgia's words. She bristled at her unspoken accusation. She didn't have to be told Lamont belonged to Grace. She would never make that kind of trouble for her.

Pam came into the dressing room as they were lining up and gave her a kiss. "Are you okay?" she whispered.

"I'm fine, baby. Go get your seat." She glanced toward the doorway where Georgia was watching her. When their eyes met Georgia smiled and moved out of sight.

As the music and procession began, Sheila's stomach twisted into a thousand knots. The shimmering lavender dress she wore lightly brushed the carpet as she walked with slow steps down the aisle. The flowers she held yielded a sweet fragrance that made her nauseous. She kept her eyes away from the crowd, afraid they would see the regret written on her soul.

Lamont and his best man stood waiting at the altar. He seemed to tower above everyone in his tux and tails, white shirt and a lavender tie. He even wore white gloves. Sheila felt a catch in her throat when she saw him. Something warm spread through her body like honey, filling every cell, muscle and limb with a sweetness that overwhelmed her. She held the flowers tighter, hoping to still the trembling of her hands. She had to make it stop before anyone saw her.

How could she hide what had always been there since the moment they met in Mrs. Gardner's kindergarten class and that lay beneath the surface of her life until this day? Her spot next to the bridesmaids seemed a thousand miles away and her shoes felt as though they were full of cement. Finally, she stepped into position and turned to look as the bridal music ushered in Grace. Everyone stood. She tried to keep her gaze ahead, but something pulled it away. She dared to look towards the men and was rewarded with Lamont's eyes locked upon her. For a split second they held, but it was long enough to declare their unspoken love.
Sheila tore her eyes away to watch Grace strolling down the aisle on her father's arm. She forced her lips into a

smile and didn't look anywhere else except Grace's glowing face.

The preacher began. Sheila listened to the words that would take Lamont away and bind him to another forever. She could walk over to him and claim his heart. She was certain he would come without hesitation. Another glance his direction bolstered her courage. "If there is anyone who believes these two should not be joined in holy matrimony, speak now or forever hold your peace." The preacher's words thundered through the silent sanctuary. They hung suspended in seconds, waiting for a response.

Sheila opened her mouth and took in a breath. The words of love she needed to declare hesitated on her tongue. They were words that should have been uttered in gentle whispers between two lovers many years ago. But the single mother had to make the good money and get everything she wanted along the way. She did it, yes, she did. She had won. She was the first Black woman at the top of her game in the banking business in this town.

She wore the badge proudly. Now she bit her tongue and bowed her head.

"I present to you Mr. and Mrs. Lamont Grier," the preacher said.

The people stood and shouted "Amen" as the couple strolled down the middle path, grinning and shaking hands.

Sheila followed, her eyes pinned to Grace and Lamont's arms locked together. She barely remembered the receiving line, the pictures and the ride over to the social hall where the reception was already in full swing. She danced and ate and drank until she was exhausted and sat down in the lobby area to cool her feet. She took her shoes off and began to rub her feet.

Pam sat down opposite her. "Mama, are you okay?"

"No, I'm not." She took the necklace off and handed it to her daughter. "Keep this."

"You're giving this to me? Why?" Pam's eyes doubled in size as she slipped it around her neck.

"I don't need it anymore, that's all. Look, go back to the reception. I'm going to grab a cab home."

"But the reception isn't over yet."

Sheila shook her head. "I'm not as young as I used to be, baby girl. I can't dance all night." She tried to laugh and gave Pam a hug.

"But Auntie Grace…"

"Auntie Grace is all right now. Go on, get back." Sheila turned away, flipped open her cell phone and called a cab. She was in the hotel lobby when she heard someone calling out to her. She turned and gasped. It was Lamont. He was the last person she needed to see and the only person she wanted to see. She wondered if Georgia saw him leave the party.

"Where are you going?" He asked, standing within inches of her.

"Home. I'm dead on my feet." She looked away from him.

"Come on. Grace wants you back. She was looking for you."

Sheila shook her head and started to turn away.

"Please, Sheila. Don't go."

The plea in his voice froze her in her tracks. When she met his eyes again, the pain in them mirrored her own. She looked around then pulled him aside.

"It's over, Lamont," she said. "I blew it."

"We can still be friends."

"No, we can't." In spite of the risk, Sheila placed a hand on his smooth cheek. "I'll always love you, honey. But I waited too long. I've got my big job, my Jag, and any piece of jewelry I want. They're going to have to keep me warm at night. Go back to your woman and give her a kiss for me, hear?"

Lamont grabbed her hand and pulled her into a hug. His warm lips touched her cheek lightly. When he pushed away, his eyes were pools of tears. Then he turned and walked back to the reception.

Sheila ran to the front of the hotel just as her cab pulled up to take her home.

What Happens in Chicago
by
Jeannette Johnson

On Tuesday morning, May 10, 2020 my eyes popped open before my brain fully woke up. As I laid flat on my back with three pillows in my bed, I looked up at the ceiling and then around the room. After trying to remember what day it was, I realized it was Tuesday. I started thinking, *what am I supposed to do today*? After about a minute it came to me. This is a day of rest for me. I decided I would just relax for another hour or two.

As I relaxed, my mind wandered. I went over my life and asked myself what had I done with my life since I retired two years ago? I should be happy and living a blessed life. I had been feeling disconnected the last few weeks. I needed to figure out why I have been feeling this way. It could be the hormonal stages my body was going through, or it could be depression. I felt like I needed to take a relaxing vacation. It had been two years since my last vacation. It was with Daisy, Lottie, and Rennie. Three good friends of mine.

Daisy is outgoing and very outspoken. She speaks her mind regardless of the situation. Lottie is the nosy one who will inquire into everyone's business. She will not stop until she gets the answer she wants. Rennie is the religious one. She will always remind you of God and will quote Bible scriptures. I am the quiet one. I am always the peacemaker because I do not like confusion or drama.

After going out to lunch to celebrate Daisy's birthday, we all decided to take a weekend trip. We discussed going to Chicago to see the play "New York And the Stranger". The play was going to be in Chicago for only three weeks. Daisy said she would take care of getting the tickets and finding a hotel. She said that she would get on it as soon as she got home. We finished lunch, paid the bill, and left the restaurant. Late that evening Daisy called and told each one the good news. She purchased the tickets and made reservations at the Golden Star Hotel. It is a new luxury hotel that was a little pricey, but we were OK with it.

A Writer's View

We decided to leave at 6:00 AM on Friday morning so we could get there and relax a day before the play. The trip was supposed to be a five-hour drive. Daisy called everyone the night before to make sure we would all be ready to go.

The next morning, she picked up everyone and we started our trip. I was in the front. Lottie and Rennie in the back. Rennie said we needed to pray before we travel on the highway. She prayed and away we went.

After about two hours on the road, the sun was shining bright. There was not much to see but lots of trees. We did see a deer run across the highway about two hundred feet in front of us.

Lottie screamed, "How fast are you going? I think you need to slow down if we want to get there in one piece!"

After that, we only saw farmland and cattle. There were large semi-trucks speeding down the highway. Rennie wanted to stop at the next service station to pick up some snacks. Daisy said there was a 24-hour restaurant about a mile ahead. "We can stop and get some breakfast," she said.

"That sounds good to me." I spoke.

We pulled off the highway on to the restaurant lot. We parked and went inside the restaurant. After we entered, the waiter took us to a table to be seated. We ordered a full course breakfast. After we ate, we paid our bill and left the restaurant.

"We ate so much food I hope we all can stay awake especially you Daisy, because you are the driver." Rennie said.

"I will put on some good music," I said, "plus I'm depending on Daisy to keep her eyes open. There are only two more hours of driving before we are there. I got plenty of sleep last night, so I'm good." After about an hour, Lottie and Rennie were sound asleep.

Finally, we reached Chicago city limits. Daisy asked me to check the address and put into the GPS so we could follow the directions to the hotel. We made it to the hotel at Noon.

"Thank God, we made it safe!" Rennie yelled.

We parked and the four of us went inside the hotel to get registered. After entering hotel, all I could say was how beautiful the hotel was. We all walked up to the desk together. Daisy spoke because she had all the information. When Daisy finished the registration, she gave each of us a key. We then went back out to the car to get our luggage. After we got our luggage, we went back inside. We located the elevator and stepped in. Before the door closed, two men hopped on and looked at each of us strangely.

"Are you ladies here alone?" One of them asked.

"What do you mean?" Lottie asked.

"We mean no harm by that, just making conversation. Well ladies this is our floor have a nice evening."

Our rooms were located on the fifth floor, which was the next floor up. When the elevator door opened, we stepped off and looked for the direction to the rooms. Our rooms were 514 and 515. Daisy and I had room 514,

Lottie and Rennie had 515. We rushed in to completely check out the room. Each room had a refrigerator and a microwave. Since we had adjoining rooms, we opened the doors between the rooms. After checking the rooms out, we discovered we were exhausted from the ride. We planned to get up around 4:00 PM. Instead, we woke up around 5:30.

"Where are we going for dinner?" Lottie asked.

Daisy responded, "Why not check out the restaurant down on the first floor. We might run into some good-looking men."

I said, "My stars, Daisy, I am not looking for men, only good food." Lottie and Rennie agreed with me. I just want to have a nice peaceful stay the next two days, see the play, and head back home. "Ok, everyone let us see what going on with the restaurant downstairs, because I am hungry."

We headed to the elevator and down to the restaurant. The restaurant had a huge dining room. It was not crowded at all, so we were able to sit where we wanted. We looked over the menu which had a variety of dishes to choose from. Daisy decided she wanted to visit the lady's room before we ordered. We said we would wait until she got back to order. When the waitress came over, I let her know that we would order when our friend returned. After about fifteen minutes, we started to worry. I told the others that I would go and check on her.

As I turned the corner to the ladies' room, I saw her coming. I yelled, "Daisy are you alright, we were all worried about you. We thought something had happened." She replied, "Oh I am fine, I will tell you about it later."

"Well, we are ready to order our food. Everyone was waiting on you."

So, we headed back to our table where the others were. When Daisy and I reached the table, Lottie asked Daisy, "Why you looking like you won the lottery."

Daisy replied, "Let's order our food and I will tell you ladies about my experience."

After we ordered our food, Daisy continued, "I

know you all are waiting to hear the news. When I was leaving out the ladies' room I was stopped by this sexy good-looking man. He was getting out of the elevator."

Rennie looked at Daisy and shook her head and said, "I need to pray for this woman because when it come to a man, she forgets everything. She did not think about us sitting here waiting on her to order our food. We were sitting here starving and she's somewhere looking and entertaining a man."

"Rennie, you don't have to make it sound so terrible. I am sorry that I had you all waiting for me."

I finally spoke and said, "Let's enjoy our dinner, then we can walk over to the outlet stores across the street."

After our meal we walked across the street. I think we walked in and out of twenty-five stores for about two hours. It was after 9:00 PM. We headed back to the hotel so we could take a shower and relax before retiring for the night. Everyone finished their shower and went to bed early, but I woke up around 2:00 AM and looked over at Daisy's bed and did not see her. I took a second look, and I thought, *well, she is in the bathroom.* I waited for about ten minutes and I still did not hear anything, I got up and called her, with no answer. I opened the door, and no Daisy. I said to myself, *"Oh no, not again."*

I knocked on Lottie and Rennie's room door and woke them up. They both jumped up in a crazy mood.

"What's wrong Cindy?"

"Daisy is missing."

"Wait, Cindy what do you mean missing? Do you mean kidnapped from her bed?"

"No, I mean-I don't know. She is nowhere in the room."

"I hope she is not a sleepwalker," Rennie said. "We need to pray for this woman because she needs serious help."

"Do you think we need to call the police? "Lottie said.

"No, we will go downstairs and look around," I said. "Maybe she went to find something to snack on."

"In the middle of the night?" Lottie replied. "Well, ladies let's go look for her. It is not a good idea to be wondering around by yourself." We put on our robes and took the elevator to the first floor. We stepped of the elevator with fear on our faces. As we stepped out of the elevator, we spotted Daisy and a man sitting over at a table near the window. We rushed over to the table.

Lottie yelled, "Daisy what is your problem! You had us worried about you. You should let someone know that you were leaving the room."

Daisy said, "I did not want to wake anyone. Sorry, you all need to stop worrying I am not a kid. I can take care of myself."

"Well excuse us for caring." I was the one who woke Lottie and Rennie up because I did not know what had happened to her. But with her attitude, I said, "Ladies we can go back up to our rooms."

Daisy stopped us by saying, "Wait before you all

go, I want to introduce you all to my friend Cody. This is the man I met when we were at dinner. We are just sitting here getting to know each other."

"We will see you back upstairs." I said in a not so nice voice.

Just as we turned to go back to our rooms, the elevator door opened and off stepped this angry looking woman with a scarf tired around her head. Her robe was flying open with her gown showing. This woman was headed our way. We looked at each other because we didn't know what she was up to. When she reached Daisy and Cody's table, she was in a mad woman's rage. We stood waiting on the woman's intentions.

The woman demanded, "What's going on here?" As she spoke again, she looked directly at Daisy.

"Will you explain to me why you are sitting here with my husband?"

Daisy stood up, looked at Cody, and yelled, "Why didn't you tell me that you are a married man!"

Cody replies, "You did not ask."

Daisy turned and looked at the lady and told her how sorry she was and that if she had known she would not have talked to him. Lottie and I walked back to the table, caught Daisy's arm and pulled her away from the table. We led her toward the elevator.

As we were walking away, we heard the lady say to her husband, "This is it, I am not putting up with you disrespecting our marriage any longer. You have done this too many times."

We were all a little angry with Daisy for interrupting our sleep. Rennie told Daisy, "Please while we are on this trip, do not look at another man. We are middle age women, and we do not need this type of entertainment."

The next day we enjoyed the play and had a nice night's sleep. On that Sunday, we enjoyed a peaceful ride home.

Well, enough of daydreaming about that trip. I seriously think the next trip will be by myself.

The List
by
Patricia H. Perry

Jack passionately kissed Myra as they lay upon rumpled sheets. Their damp hair stuck to their skin; their breathing slowly returned to normal. Jack smiled at her and then rose to dress. He slipped into his breeches and shirt all the while studying the pretty dark-haired woman reclining on the bed. Pulling on his boots, he winked at her.

"When is the ship sailing?"

"At high tide tonight," he replied.

"How long will you be gone?"

He shrugged. "Until the barrels are full of oil…one, maybe two months."

"Do you have everything you need for your voyage?"

"Well…now that you mention it, I could use a few…no…never mind."

Myra noted the hint of embarrassment crossing his handsome features. "What? What do you need, Jack?"

"Well…I won't get my share until we get back…."

"How much do you need, Jack?"

"I…umm…could you spare five gold?"

"I can spare seven gold, my love," she replied retrieving a leather bag from the nightstand. "Here."

"You don't know how much this means to me," he said taking the coins. "I'll repay you when I return."

"I'll miss you."

He sat on the bed next to her and kissed her. "Every day will feel like a lifetime without you." Myra blushed.

"Oh," he said lifting her chin up, "and no one must know about us."

"Why?"

"Because the captain will forfeit my spot on the ship."

"Why?" she asked, her head tilted quizzically to one

side.

"He didn't say, my love."

He slung his satchel over his shoulder, never noticing the piece of paper that fell out of his pocket. He opened the door, blew her a kiss, and then disappeared down the flight of stairs. Exiting the lighthouse, Jack ruffled Bard's hair as he walked past the boy sitting on the front stoop. Jack mounted his horse, glanced up at the open window, and then rode away from the lighthouse. Myra's little brother picked up a handful of pebbles from the walkway and threw them at the retreating figure.

Myra abandoned her bed. Her face glowed with emotion. Jack's passion and promises swirled within her mind. He was the one she had been waiting for her entire life. She sighed and grabbed her robe. Belting it, she spotted the paper on the floor next to the bed. Curious, she unfolded it and read the list written in Jack's neat handwriting. All of the entries had a line through them except for one.

~~The homely wench with the ample bosom at the~~

~~Crossroads Tavern: five gold~~

~~The blonde prostitute at Madam's place: nine gold~~

~~The dark-skinned singer at the Corner Saloon: nine gold~~

The simpleton at the lighthouse

Confusion rippled across her pretty face. She re-read the list, his written words exposing his true self.

This must be a mistake…he said he loved me!

The list mocked her.

The simpleton at the lighthouse…

Her buoyant emotions hovered in the air for a few moments before plummeting onto the wide plank floors and shattering into pieces.

The simpleton at the lighthouse

"You miserable mongrel." she hissed through clenched teeth.

She glanced at the women on the list. Myra knew them all…they were her friends.

"Funny", she thought, *"We don't keep secrets from each*

other so how did Jack manage to convince all of us to keep quiet about him?"

A slow, wicked smile materialized on her reddened face. She scribbled three notes and called out to Bard, who appeared moments later. He pushed a lock of reddish hair from his freckled forehead while his sister gave him her instructions.

"Deliver these to Shayree, Julette, and Brandy," she said handing him the three notes.

The boy nodded and disappeared into the growing darkness.

***

Grinning from ear to ear, Jack trotted into town. He headed to the *Crow's Nest* to meet up with his mates. Entering the smoke-filled tavern, he lifted his arms in victory over his head while his crew members whistled and banged their tankards on the worn tabletops. Jack offered them a flourishing bow and then pulled a wooden chair up to one of the tables.

"All four?" demanded a bearded man with a patch

over his eye.

"Indeed, Mutt!" replied Jack with a smirk. "And I am quite capable of doubling that before the *Night Queen* sails!"

The deckhands guffawed. One of the men slapped a serving wench on her backside as she walked past with a tray of food. She deftly cuffed his ear without tilting the tray, which elicited even more laughter from the rowdy group.

"Where's the list?" asked another mate.

Jack fished for it in his pockets. *I must have dropped it on my way here*, he thought. He held up his hands and shook his head.

"Which one was the best?" Mutt asked, his tone begging for specifics.

"Hmm," Jack leaned back in the chair as if in deep thought. "Why me of course!"

"You're gonna be dog meat when they find out about each other," warned one of his shipmates.

"But they won't."

"Why not?" Mutt asked.

"Because I told them if the captain found out he'd forfeit my spot on the voyage."

"And they believed you?!" they exclaimed as one.

Jack grinned broadly.

"Not a lick of common sense in any of those beautiful heads," declared Mutt.

"I am prepared to play a few hands," he said holding up a leather pouch. "Any takers?"

The deckhands slapped the table. He whistled while dealing the cards.

***

Myra answered the knock on the door. She nodded at the three women as they entered her home. Shayree removed her vibrantly colored shawl from around her dark shoulders. Julette's ample bosom threatened to spill out of her white blouse. Brandy flipped her blond hair over her shoulders as she sauntered in and plopped into one of the overstuffed chairs.

"What do you want?" demanded Shayree.

"I'm due at the *Crossroads Tavern* in an hour," Julette informed her.

Too busy absorbing the contents of the room, Brandy waved her hand at the other women.

"We have *someone* in common," stated Myra.

"What are you talking about?" asked Shayree.

"Jack."

"My Jack wouldn't be caught dead with a whore, lousy singer or some mousy lighthouse keeper!" stated Julette.

Shayree placed her hands on her hips. "I sing just fine, Bitch!"

"Who are you calling a whore? I'm a businesswoman who…" countered Brandy.

"…might have given him some kind of disease," Julette finished for her.

"I'm cleaner than you'll ever be!" shouted Brandy while poking Julette in her chest.

"Touch me again and I'll…"

"*Stop it!*" shouted Myra. "We were *all* tricked by that bastard!"

Glaring at each other, the women calmed down long enough for Myra to continue speaking.

"You, Julette gave Jack five gold while Brandy and Shayree each gave him nine."

"How do you know that?" asked Julette.

Myra unfolded Jack's list and handed it to Shayree. Julette and Brandy stood on either side of the dark-skinned woman and read the note. Disbelief morphed into anger.

"Did Jack also tell you to keep quiet about your romance or the captain would forfeit his spot on the voyage?"

"Yes," they confessed at the same time.

The only sound in the room was the ticking of the grandfather clock.

"He's probably gambling away our coins right this minute," stated Myra.

"That bastard," breathed Shayree.

"I worked long shifts for nearly two months to earn that money!" grumbled Julette.

"I'm going down to the *Crow's Nest* and getting my coins back!" yelled Brandy.

Shayree, Brandy, and Julette headed for the door.

"Not so fast, ladies! I have a better idea," offered Myra.

Brandy removed her hand from the door handle; all three women turned their full attention to Myra.

"I say we give him to Auntie."

"The witch?" asked a dumbfounded Shayree.

"The same," confirmed Myra.

"You know what she does to...*with*...men," muttered Julette nervously.

"That's a harsh punishment, Myra," said Shayree.

"How long has Jack been lying to you?"

Shayree, Brandy, and Julette stared at Myra, the same thought running through their minds: *A long time and a lot of gold.*

"How are we going to get Jack there?" asked Brandy after a long pause.

"We 'escort' him there," replied a grinning Myra.

"Bard?"

The boy appeared as if out of nowhere.

"You were listening, weren't you?"

"A little bit," he confessed, "but there was a lot I didn't understand."

Myra and the other women repressed a smile. Myra wrote another note and handed it to Brad.

"Let's go."

***

The group headed for the *Crow's Nest* as nightfall settled on the harbor. Brine-infused fog clung to their skin. Water lapped against pylons and hissed as it rushed onto the shore. The air was heavy and still muffling any sounds by the few people still mulling about. Concealing themselves within the shadowy alley behind the tavern, Myra nodded at Bard who ran inside and over to Jack's table. Pulling on his sleeve, the boy handed the piece of paper to a bleary-eyed Jack. A lecherous look spread across Jack's face after he read the note.

"Where is she, boy?" he slurred.

Bard pointed to the hallway leading out the back entrance.

"I…gotta go…number…number five is…waiting for me." The noise in the room drowned out his incoherent words.

Lost in their conversations with each other, Jack's shipmates never noticed him leaving.

"Show me, boy!"

Bard led him out the back and to a gloomy recessed doorway. Unsteady on his feet, Jack narrowed his eyes at the figure detaching itself from the darkness.

"Good evening, Jack."

"Myra?"

"And Shayree," the singer said.

"And Brandy," added the prostitute.

"And don't forget me," said Julette leading the horses from around the corner.

Jack took a few steps away from the women. "What…what do you want?"

Myra sprinkled a yellow liquid onto a handkerchief and placed it over his mouth. He tried to fight her off but the concoction quickly disabled him. The others searched his pockets for their hard-earned coins, retrieving what was left before Jack slumped to the ground. They tied him up and flung him face down over the saddle. The group rode up the main road and then down to the beach. Following the curving shoreline, they urged their horses up a narrow incline that led to a finger of land far above the sea. The full moon illuminated grotesquely shaped trees and brush; waves crashed against the bluff nearly a hundred feet below them on either side. The footpath tapered to a mere four feet across forcing the women to halt. Brandy yanked Jack off the horse; Julette held the reins while Myra stood near the edge of the precipice.

"Auntie!"

Only the surf smashing against the boulders broke the eerie silence.

"*Auntie!*" repeated Myra.

Tapping and scuffing grew louder as a ghostly shape materialized on the uneven span. It paused and waited for the women.

"What ya want?"

"We have something for you, Auntie," answered Myra.

Auntie glanced from one to the other and then down at the man slowly regaining consciousness.

"We thought you might want some *company*," Brandy chimed in.

"Obliged," cackled Auntie.

Auntie reached down, grabbed him by the collar and dragged him over the span without another word. Still light-headed, Jack was powerless to get free. Thorns tore his clothing as Auntie pulled him along the pebble-strewn dirt path; briars reclaimed the breach once she passed by. She finally deposited him on the plateau in front of a makeshift hut. Coming to, Jack rubbed his face and pounding temples. Looking around, he noticed a pile of bones alongside a shack. The full moon's silver light illuminated a misshapen old woman with thin white hair. Pinpoints of light peered out from within sunken sockets.

Jack struggled to his feet and backed away from the hideous creature only to trip on a branch. He groped for the bough and held it in front of him. Knobbed at both ends, he recognized the grayish white leg bone and tossed it away. He wiped his hand on his trousers and scurried backward until the wall of the shed blocked his escape. The repulsive being standing over him pointed at the piles of bones.

"Satisfy me and live; fail and you will join them."

She unhooked her cloak and let it fall to the ground. Parchment-like skin clung to her boney frame; her shriveled breasts ended in nipples resembling clumps of cold ash. His gaze focused on the desiccated emptiness between her legs. Jack's manhood fainted.

The women waited until a terrified scream echoed to where they stood. Smiling, they mounted their horses and left the womanizer to his fate. The quiet was broken by Shayree's sudden laugh.

"What's so funny?" asked Myra.

"I was just thinking where Jack will have to moor his dinghy!"

A Journey to Undeniable Peace
by
Cordelia Moye

I can't remember crying when I came out of my mother's womb. But I'm pretty sure I did. I journeyed through the birth canal with ease so I'm told. My mother said I was an easy birth, with hardly no pain at all. That was thirty-five years ago. Now instead of taking the journey of a new born. I'm taking a journey of a woman living in a world of angry and hopeless people, who is praying every day that peace will find this place called Earth. Or, that peace will bring me Heaven on earth.

My name is Eagle Brooks. My father named me that because he told my mother when I was born, I had eyes that see into eternity. Eagle eyes... I have to say, a name can be a prophecy on your life.

"Eagle I've searched for you... I prayed to find you" is what my husband said to me when we met four years ago. Before I met Solomon, I was on a walk with God that meant me being alone for some time. As other women were at a point of quiet despair losing hope on finding love or in and out of wasted relationships, I decided to stay hopeful and be patient. After ending a relationship with an ex-boyfriend that made me face the reality that, I was always picking men who were broken and abusive.

The crazy thing is that I could look at them and see it. But then I would proceed to put myself back in a place of getting hurt.

I decided to step back and take a look at myself. Which is hard to do and reconnect with who I truly am at the core. I made a decision to give myself a chance to step back and analyze what I truly wanted in my life. For peace through the madness, I would go on a journey to date God exclusively. Meaning that I would dedicate my life to getting back to my spiritual self in order to allow God to find me the right man, who would be my husband and not just a sex buddy or fly-by-night romance that would only lead to hurt feelings and me feeling used. A marriage arranged by me falling in love with myself with the help of the Highest was preferred.

I realized the reason why those relationships didn't

work was because those men could see the calling on my life. This is intimidating especially if you have good looks to go along with it. I went through the trials of loneliness sometimes. I call it a "pruning season." I felt like I was dying at times, because being alone is hard. Loneliness is one hell of a drug.

But the one thing this Eagle did was stay in the fight and kept my faith strong. One summer day, I decided to take the train to Cleveland to get away for a couple of days. At this point, I had been single for about three years and celibate as well. I was totally comfortable with traveling and doing things alone. I fell in love with quiet and calm. I fell in love with the madness of life and learned how to cope with any situation as best as I could. I was at peace, confident, and strong. When I arrived in Cleveland, I decided to head to a coffee shop after checking into my hotel.

They were hosting an open mic event that evening which I love. I'm no poet but I love those kinds of events. I had my dreadlocks up in a bun with, my diamond studs in both ears. I wore my favorite pair of boyfriend jeans with the rip at the knees with a yellow tank top that flowed and yellow sandals. Yellow is my favorite color and it complimented my deep dark complexion. I keep my make up simple.

As I drank my peach tea, a gentleman went up to the mic to perform. "This piece is called a peaceful journey," he began, which piqued my interest. When he finished his poem, he looked in my direction and gave me a nod, which I thought was odd. He walked over to me and said "Hi, I'm Solomon, the one you've been praying and waiting for." His bald head shined and his teeth were the perfect shade of white. He was tall and self-assured but I thought in that moment that he was crazy. His complexion reminded me of red clay. He had a full beard with deep dimples in both cheeks. Slender, Solomon, stood at about six feet. He was wearing a brown tunic and blue jeans with brown leather sandals. Regal looking.

"What do you mean?" I responded. I was taken aback.

"It's me – Solomon! I've been praying to God to

find me a wife that has the eyes of an eagle a woman with quiet wisdom. I know it's you... What's your name by the way?" he asked.

This was the start of our journey to an undeniable peace. Thank God.

The Paddle

by

Willie Wideman

It was September 1964, the beginning of another school year. I was enrolled in the seventh grade at Carver High School, an all-Black school in Alabama. In my small town, racially segregated schools were embedded in that time period. Civil Rights demonstrations continued throughout that year.

Despite the racial inequalities, I was excited to be back at school, with a new project to design and new friends to meet. Even though I had seven sisters, they were just my sisters. I needed to bond with girls my age.

The first day of school, in my homeroom class, a few girls were giggling, talking about boyfriends, wearing lipstick and makeup, but I was not ready for that. I was interested in finding a best friend. So, I saw a girl who sat three rows from my chair sitting alone. During the first week she told me her name was Beverly, but her conversation with me did not go beyond, "Hello." One day I asked Beverly if she wanted to have lunch with me. Without explanation she said, "No."

In math class I sat behind her, and pulled her hair in a joking manner to get her attention. She got angry. That wasn't the response that I had expected. After that she avoided me.

Days later, I noticed the boys in my class making spitballs. They took a piece of paper put it into their mouth and roll it around to form a ball using their spit. Then they threw them at the people they didn't like. I made one too, and tossed my spitball at Beverly. When the teacher came in the room, she squealed on us. We were punished with a gin belt to the hand. The teacher said "Palms up, five licks in the hand,". The gin belt was a thick strap that all the faculties used to punish students. The word, "gin belt" made reference to the belt on a cotton-gin fan. I felt the sensation of that belt for years afterward.

I often wonder why Beverly didn't want to be my friend. Just like I haven't figured out why I kept a twenty-four-inch-long wooden paddle that collects dust underneath my bed. I often wonder why I hadn't thrown it out with so many of the things that I had gotten rid of over the last thirty years, like bad boyfriends. That paddle was a high school project (Carver High School) that I finished in the Spring of 1965, which was also the year my family and I moved to Boston, Massachusetts. The paddle was designed with match sticks. I burned the top of match sticks and painted them. The back ground was blue with gold letters. I shaped the sticks to form the letters CHS in the middle. My initials were on the right and 1965 was off to the left. Over the years, match sticks have dropped off leaving empty spaces on the paddle. Every time I dust my paddle, it reminds me of special events that transformed my thoughts about the world in which I lived, including my love for sports and carrying picket signs to make a difference in the Civil Rights movement. Those were things that directly affected my life.

A Writer's View

When I was not carrying a picket sign, or working on my paddle, I found time to signed up for the girls' basketball team. The coach was there and he said, "If you miss a lay-up, you will get the gin belt." My answer was "NO" to that sport. I signed up for the school's marching band with a desire to play an instrument, but there were no instruments left. My sister, Carol, who attended the same school had already joined the marching band to play the Clarinet. I loved dancing and enjoyed it because there was no gin belt (punishment) involved. I joined as a majorette. Carol played in the marching band as I danced behind them. With both of us being members of the band, my mother, without apprehension, gave us permission to attend football games at night.

The South was and still is full of devoted football fans. Traditionally, if the visiting team was winning, the home team was prepared to fight. Well, one night our band was performing at an away game and toward the end of the game, our bandleader saw that our football team was winning. He knew it would be a fight. He ushered us out of the stadium onto the bus. The bus was safely away before the fight broke out. We never worried about gun shootings but lots of fist fighting and butts were going to be beaten, that's just the way it was at a football game.

Every weekday after school I went to the church, to pick-up picket signs to carry in town to protest. My sister and I had to go together. Otherwise, my mother would not let us participate.

We would march around the ice cream shop which was our assigned area to protest. I didn't understand why we needed to boycott it, but they said it had to be done. So, at twelve years old I did what I was told.

People were instructed to boycott (not to shop) the stores in town. We were to shop with Black businesses or designated white businesses.

One day we were on our way home from protesting in town, we saw a lady that had come from in town shopping out of the store she was told not to go. We took her groceries and spilled them in the street right in front of her. She was crying and screaming. We didn't hurt her, but she had been told! We all had been told!

Black churches played a major role in Black communities, for organizing and communicating strategies on how to fight injustice.

A church was designated as a site for a special meeting. The church members were expected to dispatch the word that an important gathering was taking place at the church on that Sunday.

Sunday at noon I walked right down the middle of the church's aisle looking at the brown wooden benches off to my right and left and its high celling. The church had sun-colored stained glass in all its windows. All the children were allowed to sit on the floor up front in the church. I remembered my sister and I were sitting, "crisscross applesauce."

We waited, and waited, and then someone said, "he's here." I looked around to see a man being escorted up to the pulpit. As he stood in the pulpit, he said, "I want to thank you for coming. We have work to do. We must come together, demonstrate and march for freedom. We cannot let what happened in Birmingham continue. We need everyone in the state of Alabama to fight." He told us exactly what had happened. I was too young to remember it all, but I was right there.

The speaker that day was Martin Luther King, Jr. I look back with reverence on the fact that I was part of that history. I met and saw Dr. King speak in-person at a time when he was making history. After his speech, the church members locked arms and begun to sing, "*I ain't gonna let nobody turn me round....*"

Days later it had been explained to me, by an adult who accompanied us, why we were demonstrating around the ice cream shop. Blacks could purchase ice cream from the windows but were not allowed to go inside to sit and order ice cream like White people. Other protesters demonstrated in front of the grocery stores, the cafe and in front of the one library in town. These places were not serving or hiring Blacks. We also boycotted stores that displayed "For Colored Only" and "For White Only," signs above public bathrooms and water fountains. I was young, so I did what I was told.

As we protested around the ice cream shop. My sister and I ignored white people yelling, "Niggers go home."

Another day after a protest march, I was taken by surprise when I had to jump out of the way of a speeding car. A white man was behind the wheel. He tried to run me over. It was at that moment that I realized that I could get killed for what I was doing.

In looking back, I am puzzled by a few people's behaviors. For instance, I will never understand why Beverly didn't want to be my friend. I don't understand how some white people can justify denying Black people the rights and freedom to which Blacks are entitled. I don't understand how some Blacks can stand on the sidelines when their rights are being violated. I don't even understand how after all these years, I kept this paddle.

What I do understand is, I was willing to die for what I believed.

A Web of Poems

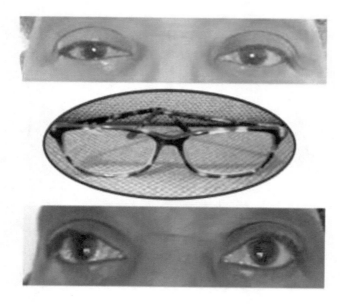

Same Eyes pays homage to **Doris Jordan Foster** who allowed me to use her eye glasses in class.

Photo: Carol Wideman

Same Eyes
by
Carol Wideman

Blackboard of blurred words
Eyeglasses made words clear
Another eyes, a call was heard

Shared with a fellow classmate
No hesitation, honored to help
The same eyes, an easy task

Words in a distant shadow
Once blurry, but now seen clearly
As light illuminating a dark room

A bridge between two lives
Unlocking words of knowledge
A pathway to incredible futures

Many years at rest on a mantle
Rejoicing of a job well done
Pride in a twofold purpose

Remembered fifty years later
warm smiles and glorious laughter
of eyeglasses that were shared

Between two with the
same eyes.

"Work Morning"

By

Elise Orringer

Fuzzy minded, heavy limbed
Counting down the T stops
A sea of face masks staring back at me on the T
What facial features are hiding beneath them?

Cell phones out in a rainbow of colors and sizes.
Passengers immersed in social media and in text...

Green line. Red Line. Bus. Walk to work.

Am the first one in.

Waiting for opening time.

Time to open up!

To him / To her

by

Vickie Wideman-Victor

You thought you were a conqueror, spider

When you caught this fly.

While you were the spider you

Spun your webs of lies.

You made this fly believe that it was

my fault you were weak.

All the time your situation was not

at all unique.

Now both spiders are the flies caught

up in the deception of your

own lies

My Normal

by

Vickie Wideman-Victor

My normal was waking up in the morning around10,
meandering in my P.J.'s like a sloth.

The pandemic has my normal, its upside down, it is
vertical. It is horizontal, it has no hours, days, months,
years go by.

Imprisoned inside my home, the warden is a 14-day
incubation of death, a germ that no one can visualize by
the naked eye, but a micro-scope.

No more engaging, Tangos replaced with a social
distancing line dance.

A mask-querade of propaganda to bring all life to a
screeching halt, the massive outcry of a grieving
communities of loved losses, a global outbreak a call to
vaccinate.

My normal is getting up again at 10, meandering in my
P.J.'s like a sloth.

Father's Day

By Christopher D.A. Wideman (Age 12)

You have worked so hard.

Today is your break.

For goodness' sake.

You are loved.

From down on earth and the ones above.

Happy Father's Day

YOUR HISTORY...

by
Lillian O'Neal

A TIME WHEN HOW OUR PEOPLE WERE TREATED AND

DARED NOT TO SPEAK ABOUT IT...

HOW WE REMAINED SILENT...

FOR IF WE DIDN'T-

WE WERE BEATEN - HUNG- WHIPPED- CASTRATED -

DISMEMBERED...

ONLY BY US RESEARCHING CAN WE FIND THE TRUTH
TO TELL IT ...

LEARN WE HAVE SOMETHING TO FIGHT- TO LEARN OUR
PAST-

HOPING ONE DAY IT WILL ALL COME OUT IN OUR
WRITING

WILL WE LEARN - WILL WE LEARN -

WILL WE PIECE OUR HISTORY TOGETHER?

WE WILL LEARN WHY POETS LIKE LANGSTON HUGHES
SPEAKS ABOUT-

"A HANGING OF TWO BROTHERS AND TWO SISTERS
HANGING ON A BRIDGE ... OF TWO SISTERS WITH CHILD
NOW MOVING JUST TO LIVE "

A Writer's View

WHY HE NAMES HIS POEM

"BITTER RIVERS "

EACH POEM HAS A BEGINNING AND AN END -

THIS IS WHY I NAME THIS -

"NO LONGER SILENT... "

THIS IS WHY I CRY MY TEARS-

THIS IS WHY KNOWLEDGE IS POWER -

"I- LILLIAN MORGAN O'NEAL TELLS YOU -RESEARCH HISTORY-

FIND A STORY WRITE ABOUT IT ...

WHO KNOWS ...YOU TOO MIGHT FIND OUT -

ABOUT "TULSA "

Much is Given and Much is Required"

by

Bro. Roland Cantwell, *A Dorchester Senior Poet*

Too much fast living

Our lives will expire.

Out grew classics of Hip Hop

Musical tunes nightmares

That follow soon by

meaningful doubts

using it to fight

A hard war and

To swear by the

Sword my lord

Or trip unseen

Pieces only more

Determined to succeed

Those have tough love

Or guessing who's missing

It will burn and turn

A Writer's View

Around those on

The ground dying

Resources in forces

Rules generally

Accepted to play by

Clues to stay high

Add dry the cosmic

Heavens make you cry

That's all is under

Makes one wonder

Much too slow

For some

Much too fast for

Others touch and

Full circle at last

Bore with details of your past

How to live only to give enough

grace my desire

To face that fire.

PART TWO - ANTHOLOGY

G&H CONSULTANT

Presents

B.FIT! COMMUNITY WRITERS

Mini Stories

AND POEMS

FROM THE VOICES OF INDIVIDUALS WITH NEUROLOGICAL STREIGHTS

In loving Memories of:

Isely Lamour
And
Alicia Patrick

Picture This!
by
Donna Barrett

Waiting in line for her morning coffee she could not decide between a latte or a cappuccino. While pondering over this major morning ritual she briefly noticed the tall casually dressed man in front of her. Removing his phone from his pocket, his wallet fell to the floor. As she started to pick it up, a small picture fell out. She glanced at the picture and was shocked to see it was a high school picture of herself from twenty-five years ago.

The picture displayed a much younger her with very long hair and slightly crooked teeth. Why would this man have her senior yearbook photo? Giving him a quick look over, he was unfamiliar to her. His curly light brown hair, green eyes and unshaven face did not ring any bells. Several emotions came over her within a matter of seconds: surprised, confused, and even a little scared. Was he someone she had dated? Could he be a stalker? Should she fear for her life? After seeing those Lifetime movies, one could only wonder.

Passing the wallet to him with one hand and the old creased photo in the other, she commented "Looks like you've been carrying this picture for a long time."

"Yes, that is someone who changed my life," he replied.

She was even more confused than before. How did I alter someone's life? She did not think she was the life altering type. She assumed it was in a positive way. Why else would he be carrying it around for all these years?

Quickly responding before he ordered and walked out of the coffee shop, she blurted, "Sounds intriguing I'm always looking for interesting stories since I am a journalist."

She could not believe the lies that had just effortlessly passed through her lips. She was not a journalist. In fact, she was an artist and a professional graphic designer for a well-known magazine.

She watched as his eyes appeared to quickly glance at her short asymmetrical haircut and then down to the whimsical tote bag on her arm. He offered to buy her the latte and said, "I can spare a few minutes if you would like to hear the story."

She jumped at his offer and immediately replied "that would be great!"

Nervously she selected a table by the window. She felt a slight comfort of seeing people walking by. Realizing she could not use her real name she quickly had to come up with an alias. The first name that popped into her head was "Charlene." After all, that was the name her mother was going to give her when she was born. But her father convinced her otherwise, arguing everyone would call her "Charlie." Mom went with her second choice.

When he got to the table, he passed her the latte and slid into the seat across from her. He appeared to be around her age. She was full of nerves and said, "Thank you. By the way I am Charlene." He nodded, sat down and stated his name. Quickly, dozens of boys from high school filled her head. It was a small school of less than four hundred students. When that failed, she started flipping through her mental Rolodex. Still nothing. She had no idea who he was.

She commented, "Not many people carry actual tangible photographs with them these days."

He smiled in apparent agreement. He proceeded to explain why he had been carrying the photo around for twenty plus years. She listened attentively as he brought her back to his first year of high school. He described himself as an introvert with a small group of friends. He would keep to himself and tried to blend in with classmates. Like most teens those were the awkward years. Adolescence was not fun for most. She continued to sip her latte with her ears intensely listening to every word. He started to tell her a story that took her back in time. A time she had not thought about in many years.

It involved a senior boy named RJ who was a bully. RJ was a football player and bigger than most of his teammates. RJ was not on the field for his intellectual knowledge. After all, as a senior, he was in the class called "Survival Math." This class attempted to teach him how to balance a checkbook, to count and to make change. On the field, it was RJ's job to block the opposing team without damaging the few brain cells he had, which were minuscule. He continued his story by describing himself as unpopular, thin, and a small teen. "I was somewhat of a geek" he stated. "Not outgoing and lacking the confidence as some other teenagers. It was intimidating just being in the crowded hall," he added. One day at the end of the lunch block, he was walking towards his next class and he was grabbed by RJ. He was frightened and tried to pull away but lacked the strength to escape. RJ held a fire extinguisher in his hand. He was thrown up against the wall and RJ pointed the extinguisher and began to douse him from head to toe. Who knows what chemicals he was being covered with? RJ laughed loudly as he aimed the nozzle towards him again. He tried to leave but was forced back against the wall. He went on to explain that just prior to being drenched for a second time an outgoing female student came around the corner. She yelled at the brainless football player with intelligent words that were way above RJ's comprehension. RJ ceased fire and returned the extinguisher to its home on the wall. He explained that this girl did not know him or his name but she obviously was kind and caring. Not only did she stop a bully from further humiliation, ridicule and possible physical harm but she made sure he was OK. She offered him dry clothes and courage. Yes, courage! Her actions gave him a new found inner strength. Her stature was small compared to RJ but that day encouraged him to become an extrovert.

He had eventually become a motivational speaker. He said, "I will never forget her name..." Just as he was about to state the name of his savior, she interrupted him and blurted "Macie!"

Dare Me Not
by
Robert 'Bob' Manning

I spent the better part of my life trying to prove to my friends how brave I was. Sadly, the effort was wasted on people who really didn't care. As I look back over some of the dares, these ones come to mind.

One dare happened when Tony, Rich, Paul and I snuck into this neighborhood club house. All of a sudden Rich made a dare, he was always making dares. Rich was a skinny blond-haired kid, a few years younger than I. His mother and father were divorced before anyone knew what divorce meant. He stayed out later than the rest of us and always got into trouble. Well, Rich dared me to eat worms. He had read somewhere about people eating fried worms. He dared me. I wanted to show him that I was brave and not afraid to try anything. I felt I was fearless, braver than any of them. So, I ate a plate full of worms. No one else would do it, so I took the dare.

There was another time when, I stopped by the

neighborhood "Packie Store" and purchased a twelve pack of Busch Beer before going to Rich's house. With beer in hand, I walked about half a mile down the railroad track to Rich house where we would spend hours in his room listening to Heavy Metal music. Rich's family owned a one-family greenhouse in Rockland, Massachusetts. Rich's bedroom walls were a pale off-white color with wall-to-wall posters of his favor rock bands and beautiful women in bathing suits. We listened to Led Zeppelin's music on his VHS for hours and later decided to hop into his 1974 Pontiac LeMans. It was rusty brown, well driven with a red and black interior. We had no fear of the "pigs" stopping us, so we decided that we were going to take a drive. We drove to the Kmart parking lot to feed the seagulls.

As a dare from my older brother, Bill, years earlier I remembered learning how to feed the seagulls bread with Alka-Seltzer pills stuck inside to watch their reaction. There I was sitting with Rich years later feeding the seagulls and waiting to see which bird would blow up and drop from the sky.

We had been drinking all day and decided to head back to my house as it got dark. Rich made a wide turn in the car and hit a large beach tree on the corner of Rice and Union Street. The front end was damaged but the car was still drivable. I got a cut on my nose but Rich wasn't even shaken up.

"Man, we don't want to get busted for a DUI, let get rid of this car." Rich said.

Rich drove the car down Cottonwood Lane straight into the woods. We walked the path in the woods that led to my back yard. Rich went home.

As I arrived inside the house, I could hear my father learning about the accident on his police scanner. Before my father could see me, I quickly cleaned off the blood from my face and changed my clothes.

My mother saw me and inquired as to what had happened, "Were you drinking?" Even though I had not admitted it she knew, and when the cops came by the house the next day asking question about the accident, my mother covered up for me.

A Writer's View

I was grounded for two weeks and Rich reported that the car had been stolen.

I am older and living my days at the Boston Home where I face many challenges. In many ways I am being faced with my biggest dares. The Covid-19 dare to live, dare to be vaccinated, and dare to wear a mask.

"Dare me not!"

Blessings
by
Lamar A. Cook

This essay recollects a monumental time in American history in which the first African American President was elected.

I was blessed to be a part of a monumental precedent in American politics. I witnessed in real-time the election process at work for the 44th President of the United States, Barack Hussein Obama.

Who was this Senator Barack Obama vying for the highest position in the land? How would he be received by the people? In a post-9/11 era, the average person lived in fear of those who looked different than them.

Critics of change were in an uproar. On the one hand, there were notably brash commentators like Donald Trump and the late Rush Limbaugh that were more brash in vocalizing the overall disdain white America felt towards then-Senator Obama.

On the other hand, white supremacist groups like the Ku Klux Klan tried to quell the growing renown and accomplishments of this Senator.

As a middle-school teacher who worked at the building where the people did all they could to vote for the next leader of the Free World, I was amazed to witness people with a myriad of ages and various levels of physical ability who made it a point to show their support of Obama, because they wanted to be a part of something amazing. Although I did not fully grasp the magnitude of what I watched that day, I was wise enough to know that I experienced history unfold in real-time.

As I reflect back, this occurrence was the nexus of what fueled my passion for the political process. Over the years I have grown to understand the plethora of routines and idiosyncrasies that encompass the democratic process of electing a President to lead the Nation.

I am continually amazed at what President Obama was able to accomplish for all Americans despite having little to no support from the House of Representatives or Congress. He had to ignore comments from Donald Trump, who spread lies about where he was born and made his time in office difficult.

Furthermore, President Obama served two terms without a single scandal, which has become a rarity in these current times and deserves applause. I'm pleased to say that President Obama's profound and admirable character remained intact throughout his years of service, and I'm thankful for what he did for America.

A Writer's View

A Father's Love
by
Isely Lamour

I want to tell you about my father and the loving relationship that we have. He will be 102 years old on November 15, 2021 and his resilience and caring nature has not changed.

He loves me and cares about me, even more so once he learned that I had developed Multiple Sclerosis (MS). He cannot understand how I developed MS when no one in the family has ever had the disease.

My father's name is Ramses. He lives in Maine with my brother. I am the eighth child of his nine children. My father speaks three languages; Creole, French and English. My father had one brother.

My father, in spite of his age, calls and checks on me every day. I should let you know that this is not unusual. Well, just the other day he called and wanted to speak with me. He calls to find out how I am doing and to make sure that my youngest sister is taking care of me.

"Where is Isely?" He would ask.

"She is fine," my sister, Carla would say.

"I need to speak to her." At that point Carla has to put me on the phone.

"How are you doing?" He would ask me.

"I'm fine," I would respond.

"What are you doing today?" he would say.

Then I would have to give him a full report of all my activities for the day.

"I want to make sure you are doing something productive."

"I am working on the computer, doing all of the exercise and most of Carla's too."

"That is good." When he says that then I know that he is proud of me.

I work hard because I want Glory at B. Fit to be proud of me too. So, I Zoom with Glory when she does her Yoga, Tai Chi and I Zoom with the Museum of Fine Arts' showcase art exhibit to let Glory know that I am serious about my activity of daily living.

My father's age is a concern for me and I worry. When two days goes by and there is no call, I become concerned about my father. He is much older and sometimes not doing well. I have my sister call him to check. I know that my sister sometime keeps his condition from me but I have to know even if I cannot do anything about his health.

No matter how the MS affects my body, I maintain a good outlook on life because of the strength that comes from my father and Glory's persistence.

There is one last thing I want to say is that I still look forward to sharing my life with another person who will love me like my father. But for the present, I am keeping him a secret. And I want you to know that he is not a, *bag of bones.*

Two Souls
by
Valencia Sparrow

Fear and confusion gazed upon

embodied peacefulness

Envying the beauty

Questioning the balance

Regretting the past

Avoiding the future

Frozen in the moment

The Search
by
Valencia Sparrow

As lights flicker

They come

crawling

Creeping up to the bar

Searching for the night's last bite

with their antennae erect

Looking for that thick, spicy sauce.

Reaching for firm onions

Investigating curvaceous jalapeños

Hey, you can't handle this

With one taste, you will flip

legs flailing, burning Icy hot

Just go!

When the Breaks Don't Come
by
Alicia Patrick

When the breaks don't come
Never before has a city seemed so cold
just sitting by the phone waiting all alone
waiting for the call ...
It says my talent has sold me a spot
Yay, I want to be a star
so, you come this far
into the final ending
I'm playing the game
for fortune and fame
without much hope of winning.

Five long and lonely years I write
scripts poems and stories
still no glory.
Filled with pain and so many tears
When the breaks don't come
I want to go back to the way
things were before,
but there's another audition tomorrow...
 So, I put away every doubt and fear
and once again I walk through the door
hoping that the break will come.

Haiku
by
Beatrice L. Zaharian

(1)

Selective repair

Every day we work harder

Smooth lotion of sun

(2)

Pinstriped Cylinder

Valleys of laced roses race

Pungency of keen

Patterns
by
Glory Wideman-Hughes

Patterns of life worn and torn
memories, feelings and emotions
deeply covering heavy woes of the world adorned.

Emotion of private squares
interlocking threads showing
 expressions quote about life.
Piercing stitches with an eye that binds strife.

A learned covering that shields my mind,
uncover life's true sheer meaning.
The beginning and things left behind
design by nature wool, felt, chiffon or cotton blend
Ripped my heart my soul, how will it mend?

Patterns of a life in many colors and forms
what is the norm?
 A style, a face for all to see
 judgment of an outer covering so let it be.

Contributors

Donna Barrett - A Massachusetts native, has a Master's Degree in Art Education. She is a former Art Educator and taught for over 20 years. Teaching kindergarten through grade 5 in the Public School System, Donna has inspired hundreds of students with her humor and her love for art.

Lamar Cook - A native of the DC/metropolitan area, was diagnosed with Multiple Sclerosis during his teenage years. After a few tears, he sought to fulfill some of his goals in life, one being an author of "Find Your Light."

Roland Cantwell - A senior/poet of Dorchester. Attended Bunker Hill college as a Fine Art major. He loves to create art work and share his poetry.

Glory Wideman-Hughes - Born in Alabama, Program Director of B.Fit! @ The Boston Home for twelve years. For over forty years she has advocated for "quality of life" for others.

Smiler Q. Wooten Haynes - Born a coal miner's daughter in Killarney, West Virginia. Migrated to Boston in 1955 and resides in the Grove Hall section of Dorchester. Member of The Historic Charles Street AME Church for over 65 years.

Jeannette Johnson - A retired Administrator from the St. Louis Housing Authority. Spent her leisure time acting in church plays. She wrote this story to share some of her creative writing.

Isley Lamour - Born in Haiti diagnosed with Multiple Sclerosis since 2002. I want to share encouraging words with others.

Robert 'Bob' Manning – Born in Roxbury, worked as a landscaper and took dares. I enjoy my life at the Boston Home and wanted to share.

Beulah Meyers - Born a Southern girl and loves to cook and dine in the best restaurants. My mission in life is to travel the world and take no mess from anybody.

Cordelia Moye - Is an accomplished poet, author and talk show host from Roxbury, Massachusetts. She's published nine books of fiction and two works of poetry. She loves working with artists and has worked the Urban World Film Festival. Her motto for life is "make life happen.... show up". Her YouTube channel is "Who's That Girl from Roxbury."

Lillian O'Neal - Was born at Claremont Park, South End of Boston, Massachusetts and moved to Hollander Street, Roxbury, when she was 5 years old. She was a Postal Supervisor for 26 years. She has won many awards and is a lover of history; you can see it in her poems.

A Writer's View

Elise Orringer - is the Generalist Librarian at the Uphams Corner Branch Library of the Boston Public Library. She has worked at the Boston Public Library for 28 years. Elise loves reading, piano playing, canoeing, and traveling.

Alicia Patrick - Born in Boston Massachusetts, and living with MS since 1992. I like sharing a joyful moment.

Patricia Perry - is the award nominated author of a fantasy series and short stories. She is a founding member of Authors Without Borders; producer and co-host of Authors Without Borders Presents... (New Bedford cable TV) and, along with AWB, has participated in numerous seminars to help aspiring writers.

Willie Wideman-Pleasants - Is an author, resident of Dorchester, Massachusetts and a graduate of the University of Massachusetts. She is a producer and host of an award-winning cable show called "Willie's Web," and a DJ at 102.9 FM's "Village" on Boston Neighborhood Network.

Colleen L. Roberts - is a loving wife, joyful mother of three, and blessed grandma of two baby girls. She resides in Brockton, MA, and writing is her passion

Alberta Sequeira - a four-times award winning author, Motivational Speaker, and an Awareness Coach on Alcohol and Drug Abuse. She is a co-founder of Authors Without Borders and a co-host of the New Bedford Cable TV. She teaches workshops on Bring Your Manuscript to Publication, and Writing Memoirs. Email: alberta.sequeira@gmail.com

Valencia Sparrow - Born in Malden, Massachusetts, a graduate of Brandeis University. She never let life get her down. She says, "I love life and I live it out loud!"

Carol M. Wideman - Is a retired Accountant, and a graduate of Suffolk University and Cambridge College. She loves history, particularly Black History. She especially enjoys passing on this knowledge to others.

Christopher Wideman - Born in Boston and enjoys writing and performing in plays. Looking forward to traveling and writing about his life's journey.

Bernice Etta Wideman - Was born in Alabama. Relocated to Boston and retired from Children's Hospital after thirty-two (32) years. An avid world traveler, a past Worthy Matron member of the Rising Sun Chapter of Prince Hall, and a member of the Daughters of Isis.

Dorothy M. Wideman - Is a Dorchester, Massachusetts resident with a Bachelor's Degree in Human Services. She loves to write suspense short stories, movie shorts and plays.

Vickie J. Victor - Is a veteran, writer, producer, instructor, and a mother of two. As one of the workshop's instructors, her experience, devotion and commitment have deepened because of all of the writers and their stories.

Beatrice L. Zaharian - Born in Boston, Massachusetts, enjoys outings, plays and family. "Love a cool sunny day."

The Sponsors:
Friends of the Uphams Corner Library
Alex E. Edwards of Thumbprint Realty
The Contributors

The contributors:
Dorchester Community Writers
 B.Fit! Community Writers
 Five nationwide writers.

Friends of the Uphams Corner Library
500 Columbia Road
Dorchester, MA 02125
Email- saveuclibrary@gmail.com

Made in the USA
Columbia, SC
07 November 2024

45354529R00072